Miss Fenella's Fault

By Bree Verity

Copyright

This book is a work of fiction. Names, characters, places and incidents either are products of the author's imagination or are used fictitiously. Any resemblance to actual events or locales or persons, living or dead, is entirely coincidental.

Copyright © 2019 Briony Vreedenburgh (Bardic Books)

All rights reserved including the right of reproduction in whole or in part in any form.

ISBN-13: 978-0-6485824-1-0

Print format

Published by: Bardic Books, 1/1 Nunyah Avenue, Park Holme, SA, 5043

This book is licensed to the original purchaser only. Duplication or distribution via any means is illegal and a violation of International Copyright Law, subject to criminal prosecution and upon conviction, fines and/or imprisonment. No part of this book can be shared or reproduced without the express permission of the publisher.

Dedication

To anyone who has ever thought they might need a fairy godmother for their wishes to come true – you don't need her. Fairy godmothers are pretty much useless.

Do it yourself. You're way stronger than you think.

About Bree Verity

Bree grew up on a diet of old movies, tea, crumpets and family values, musicals, dancing and singing. It's no wonder she writes books – it's a wonder she ever thought she might do anything else!

Bree's muses include her incredibly long-suffering partner (who has to put up with her talking through highly unlikely and probably incredibly boring strands of storyline), and two rescue dogs (who are amazed by her talent. No seriously. You can see it in their eyes.)

She is Australian born and bred but prefers the city to the rurals. Shopping and coffee instead of snakes and kangaroos, please.

Bree absolutely adores hearing from her readers, and can be contacted via her website, breeverity.com

Other Books by Bree Verity

Seven Wishes series:

Miss Cheswick's Charm

Revolution and Regency series:

The Hidden Duchess

The Misguided Mademoiselle

The Ruined Lady

The Scandalous Widow

Perth Girls series

Sax in the Park

For Business and Pleasure

Troubled by the Texan

Under the Spotlight

Bouquet of Love – an Anthology by Serenity Press

Chapter One.

The two fae stood side-by-side on the cobblestones. For the moment it was quiet, the daytime workers having shuffled their weary carcasses home for a hot meal and a long sleep, and the night workers having not yet made their way to the streets.

A person would not have seen the two fae unless they were particularly looking for them, even though they were extremely good-looking and as opposite as two people could be.

Fenella was dark haired with pale, translucent skin. Her shrewd eyes were so dark blue as to almost appear black. She was fashionably dressed, in a modest gown of dusky pink with a shawl in a darker shade thrown carelessly about her shoulders, but she moved like a black panther, sinuous and deliberate. A closer look would have revealed her featherlight wings, swaying behind her, in all their dragonfly colors.

Lachlan, as blond as Fenella was dark, had bright blue eyes and a winning smile that displayed all his white, sharp teeth. He dressed in more of a dandified style, with knee breeches of fawn, white stockings and narrow black shoes. His cravat was snowy-white, and he wore a pink jacket of almost the same shade as Fenella's shawl over a dark blue waistcoat. Fenella thought he looked ridiculous.

Lachlan either didn't notice her disdain or chose to ignore it. "So," said Lachlan. "Can you see them?"

A frown marred Fenella's smooth brow as she swept her gaze across the London street vista.

"One of them is in that house right there," she said, pointing to a large townhouse with an imposing front façade, "and I can see two others close by. And another one, maybe two or three miles to the east."

She turned her questioning gaze on her mentor as if to ask whether she was interpreting the signs correctly, but he just shrugged.

"They're your Happilys, Fenella. I can't see them."

A delighted smile crossed her face. Her very own happily-ever-afters. She was finally a fairy godmother. Albeit, with a mentor whose dress sense crossed all the bounds of garishness and back again, but still.

"Where do we start?" she asked.

Lachlan's face relaxed into an indulgent smile. "Perhaps the house right in front of us."

"Very well." Fenella gathered herself to create a spell, but Lachlan held up a warning finger.

"Remember – we want to be able to observe, but not be observed."

"Easy," bragged Fenella and, taking Lachlan's hand, they winked out of sight, reappearing in a large dressing room strewn with all sorts of gowns and under things, stockings, ribands and shoes. Two young ladies were busily preparing themselves for their evening's entertainment.

One of the young women's eyes boggled and she gave a high-pitched squeak, staring straight at Lachlan and Fenella.

Instantly Lachlan made a sigil in the air, and he and Fenella disappeared, reappearing in another corner of the room but this time, their glamour intact.

"What is it Letty?"

The young woman was still staring at the place where Fenella and Lachlan had been, her soft brown eyes popping from their sockets. She had stopped combing her brunette curls mid-motion. The other young lady, so similar in looks to Letty that she had to be her sister, had turned in her chair before the mirror and was watching Letty curiously. "I all but climbed to the ceiling with that noise you just made."

Letty took a shaky step toward where she had seen Fenella and Lachlan and pointed. "I saw a man and a woman. Right there. Just for an instant, and then they disappeared." Her voice was at once wondering and trembling.

Fenella looked abashedly at Lachlan from under her lashes, and he shook his head and rolled his eyes.

Letty's sister scoffed. "Are you suggesting we have spirits infesting the walls?"

"Oh, no, nothing like that," said Letty, but her sister had taken the idea and run with it.

"Do you think it was old Aunt Gertie who shuffled off this mortal coil only three years hence?"

"Oh, no, Aunt Gertie was short and cranky. These two were tall and handsome."

"Perhaps a pair of star-cross'd lovers who took their lives in this very room, vowing to return to each other's arms in heaven, only to realise that heaven will not allow suicides."

"Clara, you're being irreligious."

Fenella went to take a step, but Lachlan grabbed her by the arm and held her back. She scowled darkly at him, fire igniting in the depths of her dark blue eyes.

"So, were they corporeal?"

"No, they were as solid as you or I."

Fenella snorted a laugh, and a frown crossed Letty's face. Lachlan grabbed Fenella even more forcefully by the arm.

"But they were only there for an instant?" The second girl was losing interest in the conversation and turned back to the mirror and the infinitely more important matter of her hair, which she patted anxiously while peering into the glass.

Letty laughed self-consciously. "I know it is not possible, Clara, but I saw them." More to herself she said, "I could have sworn." After a moment more of frowning into the corner, she pursed her lips and resolved to put the two people out of her mind. She flicked her curls and turned back to the mirror.

Fenella made a show of wiping her brow in exaggerated relief. After making a sigil in the air to disguise their voices, Fenella said in a low tone, "It's not my fault. You know my dark magic misbehaves sometimes."

"If everyone's dark magic were as troublesome as yours seems to be," replied Lachlan darkly, "it's a wonder you all haven't reduced Byd-Tal'm to a pile of rubble by now."

She glared at him. "So, what do we do now?" she asked.

"We observe. Which one of the two is your happily ever after?"

"The one who saw us. Letty." To Fenella, Letty was surrounded by a ring of pure white light. "What are we observing?"

"We look for things that might help. Snippets of conversation. Little tell-tale signs."

"Signs of what?"

"For Rianna's sake, Fenella, did you pay no attention at all at the welcome induction?"

Fenella stayed silent. To be honest, she had not really listened at the welcome induction, preferring to glance around at the sea of new fairy godmothers, and to whisper in outrage in the ear of the fae beside her about the distinct lack of dark fae amongst them.

She opened her mouth to reply hotly to Lachlan's question, but before she could get a word in, he said, "Just be quiet."

Deep in Fenella's dark blue eyes, the tiny ruby red flame sprang to life again. She did not like being ordered about. Especially by some stuck-up light fae who obviously thought himself far above her.

Readying herself to deliver a scathing response, her action was stopped by Lachlan who clamped a big hand over Fenella's mouth. "Just shut up and listen," he hissed.

Fenella turned her flaming eyes to the sisters, vowing to get her revenge on Lachlan at some later time.

"I pray Lord Horworth is there," Clara said plaintively, still fretting with her curls in front of the mirror. "These parties are deathly dull when he is not in attendance."

"I had not particularly noticed you sulking in the corner when he was not there at any of our previous engagements," replied Letty dryly. "In fact, you seemed to enjoy the attentions of many other gentlemen in poor Lord Horworth's stead."

"I do not care to wear my heart on my sleeve," sighed Clara. "And besides, it is poor form to refuse when a gentleman asks you to stand up with him."

"So, all that dancing you do is merely martyrdom?"

Clara grinned at Letty. "Yes, that's right. It is all a terrible bore, but one must endure." She looked up at her sister from under her lashes. "Is your Captain Stirling going to be in attendance this evening?"

Letty sighed and sat down. "Yes, but we have vowed to have one dance only, so that we do not stir up any gossip."

"It is a shame," replied Clara. "You make such a lovely couple."

"I know," agreed Letty ingenuously. "Yet still Papa will not speak with James, nor give his consent to our courtship."

The two sisters sat quietly for a moment, each lost in their own thoughts until Clara sighed, gave her hair one final pat and said, "Are you ready to leave?"

"I have only been waiting for you these past fifteen minutes."

"Why did you not say so?" Clara stood, and the two of them picked up silken capes that had been draped over a chest – palest green for Letty, and powder blue for Clara, the light colors beautiful against their matching gowns and brunette coiffures.

Chattering away to each other, they swept out the door, and the candle guttered heavily behind them.

Lachlan finally took his hand away from Fenella's mouth and she scowled at him.

"You didn't need to keep it there," she spluttered. "I would have been quiet."

"It didn't seem so in the moment," reflected Lachlan. "I did what I needed to do."

"But I couldn't breathe under there."

"You seem to have survived." With a quirk of his lip, Lachlan changed the subject. "So, what did we learn about your Miss Letty?"

"That she and her sister are both of them vain, bubbleheaded nincompoops?"

Lachlan frowned and crossed his arms. "What. Else." He glared at Fenella who scowled right back at him.

"I don't know."

Lachlan sighed, exasperated. "Really, Fenella, you only have me for seven Happilys, then you're on your own. Maybe you should be taking this a little more seriously?"

"I am taking it seriously," she snapped back. "I just don't know what it was I was supposed to be observing."

"Perhaps the conversation between the sisters about how their Papa is not in agreement with Letty's choice of young gentleman?"

"Did they speak about that? I didn't hear that part at all."

"That would be a clue, would you not think?"

"A clue about what?"

Lachlan threw his eyes and arms heavenward. "A clue as to why Letty might require the services of a fairy godmother?"

"Oh."

"The girls who need our services – they're not just chosen at random you know. There's always a reason."

"What, like being kept as a kitchen slave by your wicked stepmother and stepsisters?"

Lachlan scoffed. "Where on earth do you get these odd notions? No, nothing like that. It's more like she's too innocent or too mouthy or too bookish."

It was Fenella's turn to scoff. "Oh, you mean her swains are boorish, backwater louts looking for nothing more than enigmatic creatures without a single original thought in their heads? I will guarantee to you that it is not always the fault of the young woman that the relationship does not progress the way it is supposed to."

"Perhaps not," agreed Lachlan, "but in this case, it may very well be something to do with the young lady. Something we are going to the assembly to discover."

So saying, he waved a hand across his body and changed his clothes into eveningwear – cream satin silk with a pink waistcoat and pink and gold embellishments on the sleeves of his coat. His blond hair was covered with a grey wig, tied at the back with a pink riband, and on his feet he wore golden-threaded cream shoes.

Fenella looked at him for a moment, nostrils flaring, then swept her own hand over her body. She transformed her gown into a beribboned pale-pink silk concoction. Her hair wound itself up into an intricate style, tiny diamantes winking from amongst the curls.

"Shall we away to the ball?" she asked Lachlan grandly, offering an arm. He lay a hand on her sleeve and together, they winked out of sight.

Chapter Two.

The ballroom, as was fashionable, was crowded with people, their heat and scent wafting over Letty like so much putrid perfume. She would be glad to reach the cool of the balcony.

She had been at the ball for an hour and the room had steadily grown hotter and louder. Dancing had proven to be a challenge, since it had been difficult to hear the musicians over the crowd, but at least she had her dance with Captain Stirling.

She smiled when she thought of the dashing Captain, his dark blonde hair brushed off his face, his neat moustache and beard covering a strong chin and an ever-so-slightly weathered face. His regimentals fit his muscular build well and, to Letty, he was the handsomest man in the entire room.

But now that their one dance was done, Letty was impatient to leave. There was a second party to attend, a more select and quick-witted crowd than this cattle market. But Clara was ensconced by the side of the floor, fanning herself and shouting animatedly into the ear of the poor fool beside her. This must be Lord Horworth. The gentleman seemed entranced with Clara, and Letty pitied him for the fool he was. Clara chose to bestow her favors widely (Letty clucked with disapproval); this gentleman would join the pile of her discarded lovers as soon as the next bright, sparkly object was placed in front of her.

Reaching the open double doors, she pushed through the throng of people until she reached the balustrade. Gripping it tightly, she closed her eyes and inhaled large breaths of gloriously unsullied air.

"It is rather close in there," someone remarked in a strangely accented voice near her ear and, startled, Letty turned toward the source of the voice.

"You!"

Before her stood the woman from the apparition in the dressing room. She was significantly more richly dressed, but Letty knew it was her. For a moment she thought she saw beautiful jewelled wings fluttering behind the lady, but when she blinked, they were gone.

She looked about for the gentleman that had been with the lady, but the mysterious woman said, "You won't be able to see him."

The woman's choice of words struck Letty as odd.

"Because he is not here?"

Her companion smiled and Letty very nearly let out a very unladylike shriek of surprise. The woman's teeth were lovely and white – and pointed instead of square.

In a timid voice, she asked, "Are you a vampire?"

"Of course not." The woman seemed contemptuous. "Vampires are not real. Why would you think something as scatterbrained as that?"

With a half-hearted wave of her hand, Letty replied, "Your teeth."

"What's wrong with my… oh, yes. You have those strange, square teeth, don't you?" The woman's eyes fixed on Letty's mouth. "Show me."

"Absolutely not," replied Letty primly. "It would be the height of poor manners."

"To show me your teeth? Are they that ugly?"

"No, they are not," Letty replied with some asperity. Several people turned to the source of her slightly raised voice and she flushed and returned to her normal volume. "My teeth are quite satisfactory."

"Then why will you not show me? I showed you mine." As if to prove it, the woman again displayed her terrifying, pointed incisors.

"Stop it," said Letty, flicking open her fan and holding it in such a way that both of their mouths were hidden. "Put them away."

"Why? What is so very dreadful about displaying one's teeth?"

The woman seemed genuinely puzzled, so Letty leaned in and whispered, "It may lead a gentleman to think too much about your mouth."

At the woman's blank expression, Letty blushed and continued, "To think about kissing it."

Her companion let out a loud, braying laugh, and once again Letty colored under the scrutiny of her fellow guests. Then she stopped and turned her curious eyes back on Letty.

"You're serious?"

"Of course."

"But isn't that why you're all here? Why would you create artificial barriers to the mating ritual?"

"Mating ritual?" Letty's head was spinning. Just who was this strange woman?

The woman's gaze had turned speculative.

"Since we're hiding behind your fan, there is no reason why you should not show me your teeth."

Without a ready answer, Letty threw a quick, panicked glance around – to make sure nobody was watching – and then pulled her lips back in a teeth-baring grimace.

The woman seemed fascinated, looking at Letty's teeth from several angles, peering at them as though they were some kind of museum display.

"Incredible," she breathed. "It's amazing you can eat anything apart from broth or porridge. How do you tear your meat?"

"I beg your pardon?" Letty was becoming more and more bewildered.

"Your meat? How do you tear it?" The woman gave an elaborate pantomime of picking up a joint of meat and taking a hefty bite from it with her sharp little teeth.

Letty replied faintly, "It is customary to use a knife and fork to cut one's meat, instead of tearing into it."

"Oh yes," the woman replied with a satisfied smile. "Those are what you use to preserve quetti-quette."

"Etiquette." Before the strange woman could form her next incredible question, Letty interrupted. "I do apologise, but just who are you? Why do you have such terrifying teeth? And why are you following me from place to place? It was you in my dressing room earlier, was it not?"

The woman nodded her confirmation. "All will be explained in time, dear Letty." She took Letty's hand fondly.

"You know my name?"

"I know many things about you, Letitia Caroline Rathbone. Because I am Fenella. Your fairy godmother."

Letty blinked several times in quick succession before she could answer. "Fairy godmother?"

"Yes." Fenella displayed her frightening teeth again in a wide smile, before opening her eyes wide and slapping a hand over her mouth. "Oops," she said. "Forgot."

"That's quite alright," replied Letty absentmindedly before continuing, "But… fairy godmother?"

Fenella gave a cheerful nod from behind her hand.

"And the gentleman that was with you?"

Fenella removed her hand. "My mentor, Lachlan. You see, new fairy godmothers are saddled with a mentor for their first seven happily ever afters."

"Happily ever afters?"

Fenella sighed. "Do keep up, Letty. Of course, happily ever afters. Otherwise you would not need a fairy godmother, would you?"

"I suppose not."

"So, tell me." Fenella leaned her back against the balustrade. "Who is it that would bring about your happily ever after?"

Finally, Letty found herself on solid ground. Smiling brilliantly, she said, "Why that's easy. Captain James Stirling of His Majesty's Navy."

"Ah, a captain," Fenella said, her raised eyebrow and half-smile suggesting approval. "Well, that should not be too difficult to organise. Come along to the ballroom. He is here, I suppose?"

"Yes, but…I'm not certain you understand…" Letty trailed off as Fenella pulled her by the sleeve.

"I heard you perfectly, Letty. Come along."

Reluctantly, Letty allowed herself to be dragged back into the ballroom, her apprehension tempered by a strange interest in what Fenella might be able to do about her happily ever after situation.

"Now, which one is your captain?" Fenella shouted in Letty's ear over the noise of the room.

Letty scanned the crowd, her eyes lighting up when they landed on the handsome visage of the captain. Indeed, he was half a head taller than almost anyone else in the room, it was difficult not to see him.

The captain sported a neatly trimmed and very manly beard and mustache of light brown, which matched his carefully brushed hair. Letty sighed over his high cheekbones, which bore just a wisp of blush as if an angel had kissed him. And speaking of kissing, his lips were full and, at the moment, moving fast as he engaged in conversation with the other officers in his group.

His wide shoulders were the perfect hanger for his military jacket, with its high collar and shining epaulettes.

And although she could not see them from this far across the ballroom, Letty knew that his eyes were a perfect, intelligent green.

"He's over there," she said, "the tall man. Only I must tell you…"

"Come on," said Fenella, ignoring Letty's words and once again grabbing her by the arm. This time Letty resisted.

"You do not expect us to simply saunter straight up to him?"

"Well, how else are you going to ask him to dance?"

"Ask him to… I shall do no such thing!" Letty was aghast. She pulled her arm out of Fenella's grasp and sat on a nearby chaise.

"I don't understand," complained Fenella, plopping down beside her.

"Two unattached ladies cannot simply… stroll up to a circle of gentlemen! Imagine how we should look."

"How should we look?"

"Like a pair of shameless hussies, that's what." Letty crossed her arms over her chest.

"Then how do you ever get to know them?"

Letty could not believe the confusion in Fenella's expression. Crossly, she replied, "You wait to be introduced of course, and then once you are introduced, you wait for the gentleman to approach you."

Fenella rolled her eyes. "And this is all part of your quetti-quette thing as well?"

"Etiquette." The word came out of Letty's mouth as a low growl.

"Well if that doesn't sound like one of the most foolhardy things on this version of Earth, I don't know what it is." Fenella reached into her reticule, still grumbling to herself. Letty tried not to be interested, but when Fenella's entire hand disappeared into the tiny bag, and then half of her lower arm, she turned, her mouth falling open.

Fenella's eyes twinkled and she dove in up to the elbow. "Ah, there it is," she said, her face lighting up. "I knew it was there somewhere."

When Fenella pulled her arm back, Letty saw she held a butterfly made from pink folded paper. It was flapping its wings in a frenzy, trying to escape Fenella's grasp.

Letty shook her head. The paper butterfly was trying to escape?

"Stop it," Fenella said firmly and enclosed the butterfly in her two hands. She whispered some strange words into them from no language Letty had ever heard. Then Fenella opened her hands wide and the butterfly flew away.

Letty watched it meander its way over the heads of the heedless crowd until it arrived over Captain Stirling. In silent fascination, Letty saw the butterfly pop and turn into a dozen pink bubbles that drifted down to the head and shoulders of Captain Stirling before disappearing on impact.

He immediately turned and caught Letty's eye.

"What did you do?" Letty said nervously to a smug-faced Fenella.

"I have called him to you."

"Oh no."

Captain Stirling arrived in front of her at just that moment. He bowed slightly, and said, "May I have this dance Miss Rathbone?"

"No," she hissed.

He stood up straight and blinked twice. Then, he made the exact same bow as before and repeated, "May I have this dance Miss Rathbone?"

"I said no, James. Go away. You're making a scene."

Letty unfurled her fan sharply and fanned her face.

James stood up straight again and blinked twice again. He bowed. "May I have this dance, Miss Rathbone?"

"You might as well accept," offered Fenella. "He's not going to stop until you say yes."

Letty glanced around desperately for a way out, supremely conscious of all the eyes on them, then with a belabored sigh, she took the Captain's arm and he led her to the floor.

Lachlan sauntered up to Fenella and handed her a glass of champagne. She clinked it against Lachlan's glass absently and took a sip, her eyes not leaving Letty and her captain.

"What is it?" asked Lachlan. "You got them together. That's half the job done."

"Yes, but they're supposed to be staring blissfully into each other's eyes," Fenella fretted. "They aren't even talking. And Letty looks like a thundercloud about to burst."

"And the fellow seems to have just found himself in a horrible nightmare, by the look on his face," Lachlan mused. "What did you do wrong?"

"Nothing." Fenella turned on him. "Why would you think it was me? Is it because I have dark magic instead of light?" Before Lachlan could defend himself, she continued. "It's these impossible humans, Lachlan. They never behave how they are expected to. They're supposed to be gazing adoringly at each other."

"Instead, they look as though they would both of them prefer to be anywhere but where they are," Lachlan agreed.

"Perhaps he isn't the one?" Fenella suggested, but Lachlan shook his head.

"No, it's all there in the auras. Can't you see it?"

"You know my skill with auras is practically non-existent."

"Yes, we'll need to work on that. But take it from me, he is definitely the one."

"What could possibly be wrong then?"

He shrugged. "I don't know. But I doubt that we will be able to figure it out tonight." He downed the rest of his champagne. "We should probably return to headquarters and regroup. Come up with a new plan of attack."

Fenella sighed. "And I didn't even get to have one single dance."

Lachlan threw her a rueful grin, then grabbed her hand and they winked out of sight.

Chapter Three.

Letty stood as still as she could, hands clasped demurely in front of her to keep her Papa from noticing that they were shaking. She had known this interview would come, as soon as she stood up with Captain Stirling for the second time.

That foolish fairy godmother! Did she know nothing about the proper way to bring about an attachment? It certainly was not by rushing up to the gentleman in question and forcing him to take one's hand.

And yet, Letty recalled, Fenella had looked mightily pleased with herself as she watched Letty and Captain Stirling cross the room barely looking at each other. She obviously did not understand the significance of a second dance. Heaven knows what might have happened if she had forced a third on them!

Crash!

Letty's thoughts returned to the present as her Papa banged his goblet down on his desk.

"I thought I had made myself perfectly clear, Letitia," he said, cold fury seeping from his tone.

"Indeed, you had, Papa," replied Letty, eyes downcast, hoping that the slight tremor in her voice had not been noticed by her Papa.

"And I am unaccustomed to my direct orders being disobeyed in such a flagrantly disrespectful way."

"There is an explanation Papa…"

"Explanation?" he sputtered in Letty's face. "Explain how I have done nothing this morning but receive well wishes from a hundred of my acquaintances about finally marrying off one of my girls."

"Well, you see, Papa," Letty began earnestly, but her Papa interrupted.

"Oh, I'm certain you have some quick-tongued reason for it happening, Letty, but that does not matter." Her Papa grasped her around the shoulders, a little tight, and Letty gasped.

"You will not pursue a relationship with that blackguard, do you understand me?"

Letty felt obliged to defend her captain. "He is not a blackguard, Papa, he is a captain in His Majesty's Navy…"

"If I say he is a blackguard, then that is what he is, you uncompromising young chit."

Letty felt it prudent to hold her tongue.

"You will not dance with him ever again."

Letty gasped, prudence forgotten. "But that is unfair, Papa. All gentlemen are entitled to one dance…"

"Not this one." Her father held up a finger. "I see you in one single embrace with him and you will be packed off to a convent quicker than you can say Jack Frost. And that goes for your sister as well."

Letty's head spun. No more dances with James? How else were they to prepare their secret wedding? Clandestine meetings in darkened gardens? Letty's lip curled at the distastefulness of such an action.

Her Papa took her curled lip as yet another instance of his daughter's insolence. "You had better take that face away from me, girl," he warned.

Letty's jaw tightened. "I shall relieve you of my presence at once, sir." Stiffly, she left the room, mustering every ounce of hauteur she could, before upon leaving the room, breaking into a run that took her to the parlour where she knew Clara would be.

One look at Letty's woebegone face was enough for Clara to leap out of her chair and take her sister by the hand, leading her to her favorite chaise.

"It did not go well then?"

"Indeed, it did not." Letty blinked back tears. "He wants me to have nothing more to do with James."

Wide eyed, Clara asked, "What are you going to do?" As she spoke, Clara deftly picked up a cup and saucer and poured a hot cup of tea, which she passed to Letty, who accepted it with the same practiced manoeuvre.

"I have no idea," Letty sighed, sinking into the chaise.

"What on earth made James approach you like that?" Clara said, running her eyes over a selection of small cakes and picking up a pink confection, sniffing it before popping it in her mouth.

Color bloomed on Letty's cheeks. "Clara," she began unsurely, "Do you believe in magic?"

Clara stopped chewing. "What does that have to do with anything?" Her voice was thick with cake.

"Well, what if I were to tell you it was magic that made James approach me?"

"I should say that you definitely take less champagne at our next ball. Magic indeed." Then, stricken for a moment, she turned to Letty. "There will be another ball, right? Papa did not…?"

"No, he did not banish us or put us under house arrest or anything. He did threaten to send us to a convent though."

"An empty threat," Clara declared confidently after a moment of thought. "He knows no convent on any of the continents would have me."

"Clara, please do concentrate." Letty waited until her sister's gaze once again lie on her, and repeated, "Do you believe in magic?"

"No."

"It sounds absurd, I know…"

"Wait just a moment. Are you telling me that you DO believe in magic?"

Letty shrugged helplessly. "Up until yesterday I would definitely have said no. But I swear to you, she used some kind of enchantment to entice James to come to us."

"She?"

"My fairy godmother."

Clara took Letty's forearm gently. "Are you still feeling the effects of last night's champagne, darling? Let's get you to bed, shall we?"

Letty shook her off. "No, Clara, this is serious. I have a fairy godmother. And one whose meddling so far has very nearly cost me the love of my life."

"A bad fairy godmother then?" Clara sat down beside Letty on the chaise.

"No, I don't think so. Just an ill-informed one."

Clara still looked sceptical, and Letty produced a soft laugh. "I know it sounds insane, Clara, but you are the one person I need to believe me."

The sisters looked at each other and Clara replied, "It is difficult to do Letty, since it is so fantastical. But," and she squeezed Letty's hands gently, "I do believe you."

Letty sighed in relief.

Clara said, "So, what happens now?"

Letty shrugged. "I suppose James and I continue to meet clandestinely until we can work out a way to overcome Papa's objections."

"And all the while making sure this fairy godmother of yours doesn't destroy all of your chances?"

"Exactly."

The two sat with their elbows on their knees and their fists under their chins, brows drawn down, thinking hard.

Fenella watched from the other side of the parlor window. Lachlan, too, stood beside the window, only his attention was upon the sheaf of transparent papers in his hands. Fenella turned to Lachlan.

"So," Fenella said, "do we know what Papa's objections are?"

Lachlan looked up from the papers. "No, but you had better hurry up and find out before Letty's happily ever after is lost forever."

"Me? But you know how much I hate the research."

"Fenella, you knew research was part of the job when you took it."

"But I didn't think I'd have to be in those smelly old archives every single day.' She brightened and clicked her fingers. "Can I not just hit the old man with a compliance spell?"

"A compliance spell is only temporary."

"Long enough for them to get married?"

"You can only use your magic on the subject. You've already skirted a line with the summoning spell above James Stirling's head."

"It hardly even touched him."

"Fenella…" It was impossible to miss the warning note in his tone, but Fenella chose to ignore it.

Eyes bright, she said, "I could get Captain Stirling to do an Act of Derring Do! That would endear him to Papa."

"You would be much better to do some research…"

"I know," said Fenella, clearly ignoring Lachlan. She clicked her fingers and was gone.

Lachlan sighed deeply, yawned expansively, then went back to the sheaf of papers in his own hands. "I hope you know what you're doing," he muttered.

Chapter Four.

With Clara's assistance, Letty had been able to meet with James on a semi-regular basis in a quiet area of Green Park, where there were no horses and little foot traffic. A stream that usually meandered alongside the path was choked with weeds it seemed and had settled into several oily-looking and bad-smelling ponds, which drove the crowds away. Today as they walked, Letty did not even notice the stench. She was too busy chiding James for his behavior at the ball.

"I cannot apologise enough, my love," said James, earnestness shining from his eyes. "It was as if some otherworldly sensation came over me and I was no longer in control of my body. Believe me, I was every bit as mortified as you when I realized we were dancing together for the second time."

"Could you not have fought it?" asked Letty. "That otherworldly sensation?"

"My mind was not my own until I came back to find myself dancing in your arms. I suppose I owe an apology to Colonel Dartford too – our conversation must have ended quite abruptly." James gave a sudden cheeky grin that brought youthfulness to his features. "However, I will admit, spending an additional twenty minutes in your arms was not a terrible experience." He brought her hand to his lips, holding eye contact with her, his grin not wavering.

Her cheeks bloomed and she smiled, but said with some severity, "But now Papa has forbidden us from dancing at all."

He was instantly contrite. "What was I to do? I had no control. It was most unsettling."

For the second time in days, Letty asked a question she never expected to need to ask of anyone. "James, do you believe in magic?"

"You mean parlor tricks? That sort of thing?"

"No, I mean real magic. Unexplainable things."

James considered for a moment. "There are many superstitions aboard ship in the navy," he said. "But until the ball I will admit, I had never personally had experience of anything of a supernatural nature. But," he cautioned, "I'm still not certain. It may have been some kind of brain injury or megrim or something."

"What if," Letty said carefully, "I was to tell you that the spell on you was cast by my fairy godmother?"

James laughed aloud, a merry, musical baritone but sobered when he saw Letty's woebegone expression. "Are you in earnest?"

"Yes," replied Letty miserably. "I have a fairy godmother."

"That you do."

Letty and James sprang apart as between them, Fenella appeared, twirling a small pink parasol.

James goggled at Fenella. "But... but you just appeared," he said disbelievingly.

"Yes."

"Out of thin air."

"Yes. That's how I always appear."

"And... and... your wings!"

She flapped them once with an adoring look over her shoulder, then they disappeared.

Beaming at their twin bewildered expressions, Fenella turned to Letty. "I have another idea about how to bring about your happily ever after."

"No thank you," replied Letty emphatically. "You have done enough. Quite enough."

Fenella's expression fell for a moment, but then a grin crossed her face. "But you do not have your happily ever after yet. So, Captain Stirling, you need to do an Act of Derring Do, to win over Letty's Papa."

"Pardon me?" James was still contemplating Fenella's arrival. She sighed heavily.

"Come along, James. It's time for you to prove to Letty's Papa you are heroic and caring."

"And just exactly how is he supposed to do that?"

Before anyone could say another word, Fenella gave Letty an almighty shove, sending her headlong into one of the grubby, smelly pools of water by the walkway.

James stared at Fenella in horror before she gave him a little push in Letty's direction. "Go," she encouraged. "Save your lady."

James, springing to action at Fenella's words, pushed her out of his way and looked to find Letty seated in six inches of boggy water, her hat sagging down over her bedraggled curls.

"James," she said plaintively, and James stepped into the shallow pond, mindless of his boots, to lift her out of the water and set her on her feet.

"You smell as fusty as Jacob's pig farm," he remarked, earning himself a glare from Letty.

Shivering and stinking, she looked for Fenella, but the only people approaching were Clara, her expression incredulous, and several other groups of people running up from all directions, asking her if she was alright, commenting on how unlovely she smelled, taking her sodden shawl and replacing it with a lovely warm woollen one, and calling for a carriage.

Letty stared at James the whole time, not seeing or hearing the people roundabout, but only seeing her own bereft expression copied in his face. Once her Papa found out about this escapade – and he would find out – he probably would put her in a convent, and she would never see James again. No words passed between them, but in that moment, Letty felt her heart shattering.

The carriage arrived and Letty and Clara were bundled into it along with a buxom woman - who had taken charge of the poor shivering Letty - and her mousey companion. When James tried to ascend the step as well, the buxom woman said stridently, "Have you not done enough damage for one day young man?" and pushed him away, shutting the door in his face.

She ascertained Letty and Clara's direction and after shouting it to the coachman, settled back into the cushions of the carriage and asked, "Lover's tiff, was it?"

"I beg your pardon?"

"The reason your gentleman pushed you into the pond. Was it a lover's tiff?"

"No! James and I never fight. It was my fairy godmother's fault."

The buxom woman exchanged eloquent glances with her companion and took up one of Letty's hands.

"It is quite alright, my dear. Men sometimes do not know their own strength."

As Letty stared at the woman, Clara took up the refrain.

"But James would never do such a thing."

"There was nobody else there, dears. Unless you tripped and fell into the stinking hole?"

"My fairy…" Letty's words died as she realised what she was saying. "There was another woman."

"There always is," the mousy companion said in a nasally, thin voice that matched her looks. She sniffed and pulled her dark shawl closer around her.

"No, I mean walking with us," insisted Letty.

"No," the buxom woman said doubtfully, "there was nobody else there. It was only you and the young gentleman. I saw the whole thing."

Letty allowed the woman to fuss over her until they arrived home, where Clara marched Letty inside and ordered a warm bath and dry clothes. Letty thanked the buxom woman for her kindness.

"It was nothing my dear," the woman said. "We women must stick together when our men misbehave. I hope I can get the stench out of my carriage seats! Toodleoo!"

Hurrying Letty upstairs, Clara demanded, "Tell me everything. I did not see Fenella there either."

As she shed her wet clothes and put on a warm robe while they waited for the bath to be drawn, Letty told Clara what had happened. Clara's mouth tightened.

"I pray word of this does not make it to Papa's ears," she said. "For if it does, you can kiss your clandestine walks goodbye."

"And then I will not see James at all," Letty agreed forlornly. "I cannot imagine how Papa could not hear about it, can you?"

Clara shook her head. "No. After all, it is not every day one's daughter is pushed into a pond in Green Park by the very man she had been instructed not to see," she mused. "It is a most unusual occurrence and one, I suspect, that shall be on the lips of many people in a very short period of time."

"What am I to do?" sighed Letty.

Clara could only shake her head sadly as the footmen brought in the deep copper bath. "We shall figure something out," she said confidently, although Letty noticed that her confidence did not reach her smile or her eyes.

The arrival of James the following morning for a meeting with Papa did not bode well either. Letty and Clara could hear them thundering at each other from the parlor, where they waited hand in hand.

Letty attempted valiantly to keep her tears at bay, however listening to the two men she loved most in the world bellowing at each other seemed suddenly enough to have her bursting into hysterics. She pulled her hand from Clara's grasp and put both of her hands over her ears. Clara wordlessly put an arm around her shoulders.

They seemed to argue for hours – for a moment there would be a lull and Letty prayed it was over, then one or the other of them would raise their voice again, and the nightmare would restart.

Letty was glad for the comfort of her sister's arms as she waited, white-lipped, for the men to finish. Every now and then Clara would drop a light kiss on Letty's hair and whisper, "Be strong, sister." They were the only words either of them spoke during the entire hour-long rampage.

Finally, a door slammed, and Letty tore herself out of her sisters embrace, racing to the doorway to look out into the wide entrance to the house.

James, his face white, strode from the study to the front door, catching Letty's eyes for a moment before dropping the contact as he walked away.

Letty's heart dropped. In his glance, Letty felt all of his love and pain. He didn't offer her even the most fleeting of smiles, or a flicker of a wave or anything. Letty knew what it meant, and dreaded to hear it, but had to be certain.

Rushing to her father's study, she wrenched out, "What did you do?"

Her father stopped in the middle of opening a fat ledger.

"That is hardly the correct way to address your father," he said mildly.

But Letty was in no frame of mind for a lesson in honouring your parents. Her breathing erratic and her eyes hooded, she took a faltering step into the room before repeating, rather more sternly, "What did you do, Papa?"

He looked up at her from under heavy brows. "I did what any good father would have done under the circumstances. I told him never to try to speak to you again."

"No!" The anguished word burst from Letty's lips. She grasped the back of a chair, certain that her knees were about to collapse under her.

"What else was I supposed to do, Letitia? Not only were the both of you blatantly disregarding my express instructions, but I also hear from several sources that you and he were arguing furiously in a public park and that he proceeded to push you into a pond. I ask again, what else could I have done? The man is a bounder and I will not have him sniffing around my daughters."

"He is not a bounder," Letty replied hotly. "He is good and kind and would never do such a thing. You just need to get to know him."

"Know him? I sent him away with a flea in his ear."

"But he did nothing wrong."

Her father quirked an eyebrow at Letty. "Clandestine meetings? Walking alone in the park with an unmarried young woman? His behavior skirts the boundaries of good manners."

"If you had allowed us to walk out normally, we would not have needed to…"

"Enough!" Papa's fist came crashing down on the desk. "I will not be made to be the ogre in this scenario. You did not obey my direct instructions."

Letty glared at her father, her tears drying to cold fury on her cheeks. He glowered back at her, the exact same expression on the face of both father and daughter.

"I will not allow a dalliance with anyone of that family. And since you cannot seem to follow that one simple instruction, from now on, you will not venture outside the walls of this house without me."

"Papa!" Letty was aghast. "No!"

"It is your own fault, Letty. I warned you of the consequences of disobedience."

"But I love him." The words fell easily from her defiant lips. Her father's eyes narrowed.

"I am certain you believe it to be so," he replied stiffly. "However, time will prove, you are most certainly not in love. Not with that boy."

Letty wilted like a peony on a thin stalk. "It is too love, Papa," she whispered. "And I shall never get over it, not in a million years."

* * *

Clara discovered Letty half an hour later face down on her bed, her pillow sodden with tears.

Even the comforting pressure of her sister's hand rubbing her back did nothing to lessen Letty's misery.

"When did he become so cruel, Clara?"

"I wish I knew," Clara sighed. "He was never the most demonstrative of parents, but he never refused something that was so patently important before."

"What does he have against James?"

"Again, I wish I knew."

Letty sat up to face her sister, her eyes red and swollen. "He said something odd to me, Clara. That I would never be permitted a dalliance with anyone in that family. What does that mean?"

"With the family? Are you certain that was what he said?"

Letty nodded miserably. "It matters not, really, what he meant. Either way, I never get to see James again. Do you know, he even refused to believe that I love James?"

"Is he blind?"

"What am I to do? How can I survive without James?"

"You need not."

Fenella winked into sight in the centre of the room, to very different reactions from each sister. Letty groaned, while Clara stared open-mouthed at Fenella.

"Where did you come from?" she asked, astonished.

"I was just outside," replied Fenella airily.

"Well, you can just take yourself back outside," said Letty grumpily. "I have no wish for any more of your interference."

Clara still goggled. "But you just... appeared in the middle of the room."

"Yes. Fae can transport."

"Fae?" Clara squeaked, and Fenella turned on Letty.

"You haven't even told her about me?"

"Of course I have," replied Letty crossly. "And how you have been nothing but trouble."

"Nonsense," said Fenella briskly. "I have worked to bring matters to a head. You all knew this confrontation would occur sooner or later. I have merely… speeded up the process."

"I wish you would speed yourself out of here."

"Now Letitia, is that any way to speak to your fairy godmother?"

Clara got off the bed and came over to Fenella, fascinated. "But you look just like any other person," she marvelled, circling the fae. "Did I not see wings when you arrived?"

"Yes, but they tend to distract humans, so we are instructed to hide them."

"May I see them?"

Fenella smiled and her beautiful jewelled dragonfly wings appeared, but Clara blinked and backed away.

"Those teeth." She shivered.

Fenella put her wings away as Clara continued, "And your purpose here is to assist Letty to find her own happily ever after?"

"That's correct."

"And just how do you propose to achieve that now that James and Letty are not permitted to speak to each other?"

"And," added Letty acidly, "since I am not permitted out of the house unless I am under the chaperonage of my father?"

Clara turned her head toward Letty. "Really?"

Letty confirmed with a nod, and the two sisters turned back to Fenella.

"I have a plan," replied Fenella, a little uncertainly.

"Do let us know the details," replied a frosty Letty. "I can only imagine the delights you have in store for me. Am I to be flung off a horse? Pushed off a precipice?"

Fenella held up her hands before the two accusing sisters. "I merely wanted to let you know I have the matter in hand," she said. "You need not worry, Letty. Your happily ever after is assured." And with that, she winked out of sight.

Letty rolled her eyes as Clara remarked, "I wonder how she does that."

***

"What am I going to do?"

Fenella paced restlessly before Lachlan who was seated at his desk, hands clasped, watching her calmly. She really did resemble a hunting panther, coiled tight and ready to spring at a moment's notice.

"Did you do your research?"

She threw him a sour look. "You know that I didn't, Mr Smarty Pants."

"Then it's lucky for you that I did."

Lachlan picked a thin sliver of plastic up from his desk. It seemed to be transparent and all colors at once. Wordlessly, he held it out across the desk to Fenella.

She goggled at him for a moment, before snatching the sliver from his hand and plopping down into a wooden chair, relief on her face. Murmuring a few choice words brought a bright display to life on the plastic. She started to scroll through the information.

Lachlan interrupted her search. "There's some very interesting material on there about Letty's father that you may wish to share with her. A past love gone wrong."

She glanced up at him, then back down to the sliver. "Will it change his mind about Letty and James?"

"It could, used judiciously."

"It must be very juicy," Fenella said absently, still looking at the display.

"I would suggest you study that thoroughly before you do anything else." Lachlan's tone was peremptory, but it didn't intimidate Fenella. She glanced up at Lachlan again, a beaming smile on her face.

"Oh, I will." Fenella stood, radiating joy. "Thank you for this, Lachlan. I promise I will make it right." With that she whisked out of the room, dark hair flying behind her.

Lachlan sighed, watching the space where Fenella had been. What was he doing? The whole point of fairy godmother training was for the fae to learn the techniques, research being one of the most useful tools of all. But Fenella had only to throw him her cheeky smile and look at him with those dark eyes and he was off doing the work she should be doing.

It would not do. His job was to mould the dark she-fae into a functional, practical fairy godmother. And even if he had to fight his own instincts to do it, that's what he would do.

With another sigh, he returned to the multiple papers on his desk.

Chapter Five.

Tap tap tap.

Letty awoke, groggy and disoriented. She glanced about through heavy-lidded eyes, unsure of what had awoken her. The flames burned low in the fireplace grate, but nothing else moved in the room. Letty pulled the covers higher up on her shoulder and settled back down to go to sleep.

Tap tap tap.

She sat up in bed with a start, this time fully awake. The tapping had come from her window.

Puzzled, intrigued, and more than a little frightened, she tiptoed over to the window, holding her breath. Then before her quailing nerves could fail her, she flung back the curtain, only to find James' smiling face staring at her through the window.

With a cry she pushed up the sash and James tumbled into the bedroom.

"Shh," hissed Letty. "James, what are you doing here?"

James scrambled to right himself, standing before Letty with an expression of half-guilt, half-defiance.

"James?" Letty said again. "What have you done?"

"Stolen away from my crew so that we may be married."

Letty stared at him for a solid half minute. He shuffled his feet a little and laughed self-consciously, ducking his head to run a hand about the back of his neck.

"Well, that was not quite the response I expected."

"Of all the scatterbrained, half-witted… truly romantic things you have ever done, James Matthew Stirling, this certainly takes the cake."

James' face, which had fallen at the start of her words, broke into a smile and he lunged at Letty, picking her up in a whirling embrace.

"You are quite mad, that's what it is," she said, hands on his shoulders and looking down at him lovingly.

"That I am, miss, mad in love with you." He returned Letty to her feet and, grasping her face in his hands, planted a long, sweet kiss on her willing lips.

Letty sighed, comfortable in his arms, but aware of a dreadful nagging in her brain.

"I cannot wait for the day I never have to let you go at all, Letty," James said from somewhere close to her ear and the implications of the words brought a sharp burst of color to Letty's cheeks and an impish smile to her face. She took a step back and looked at him from under her lashes.

"So," James said eagerly. "Pack up your things. I can help you. Our journey to Gretna Green begins tonight."

"Tonight?" Startled, Letty allowed her grip on James' shoulders to falter. "I cannot go tonight."

"Why ever not?"

"Well, there is my family for one thing. Clara would never forgive me for getting married without her in attendance."

"I think Clara will understand, given the circumstances," replied James wryly.

"And my clothes. I cannot just pack up my entire wardrobe in ten minutes."

"You do not need your entire wardrobe, Letty. Just enough for a few days to get us to Gretna and back."

Letty could hear the stress in James' voice, and she sat down on the chair by her little dressing table.

"Oh, James, I just do not know."

"Letty," said James, and she looked up at him as he took her hand. "I expect to be in plenty of trouble for doing this, but I thought it would be worth it because I would finally be married to you. And I thought you would be as excited by the prospect as I."

Letty knew she was disappointing James, but something inside her stopped her from being able to be as excited as he.

"But Gretna," she said plaintively. "Is it not just a little… common?"

"I believe you mean dashing and romantic," James corrected.

Letty thought of a highly uncomfortable four-day carriage ride coupled with shady posting inns where strangers would wink at her, knowing what she was up to, and the women who would throw their disdainful glances at a ruined girl whose only chance now was to trap her fellow over the anvil… and she realised she could not do it.

"I cannot," she whispered sadly, dropping her eyes.

"I beg your pardon?"

"Oh, James, you know I love you more than anything else in this world. But I simply cannot do it. It would not be right."

"But it's the only way, Letty. Your father has forbidden me from even speaking to you."

"Then we must change his mind, James, you and I, instead of careening all over the countryside and returning a laughingstock."

James took a step back. "Is that what you really think Letty? That we would be a laughingstock?"

Letty's mind was fast swimming away with her. "No, James, of course that's not what I meant…"

"Then what did you mean? I do believe I should like to hear what it really was you meant."

"Oh, I do not even know, James, the whole thing is giving me the megrim." She put a hand up to her forehead in what she hoped was a forlorn, weary gesture and peeked out from between her fingers only to find James regarding her with bored impatience. She sighed and dropped her hand to her lap.

"Can you not see? The circumstances of our marriage would follow us everywhere we went. We would never live it down. The legitimacy of our children would be questioned," she put a hand over his protesting mouth, "even though we would know for a certainty they were born in wedlock. I could never look the bishop in the eye again." She shook her head. "No James. It is simply not something that I can do."

"So, you do not wish to marry me then?" James was playing down his hurt by sounding belligerent, but Letty knew she had cut him to the quick.

"Of course I wish to marry you James."

"Just not enough to stand up to a little public censure."

Letty was silent. There were no words to respond to James' accusation. She looked up imploringly into his eyes, but he was already making his way across the room back to the window.

"Well, do let me know if you change your mind," he said frostily, climbing out and on to the long ladder he had propped up against the side of the house.

Letty rushed to the window. "Do be careful James."

James sniffed. "Pretending that you care now, is it?"

"But I do care," she implored.

Just before his head ducked below the window, James looked directly into Letty's eyes and said, "Just not as much as I do about you."

Letty closed the window and the curtain before throwing herself on the bed and once again drowning her pillow in tears.

* * *

Fenella, unaware of the drama that was taking place upstairs, knocked on the front door of Lord Rathbone's home, patting her newly blonde hair back and noticing the heavy, sweet scent of Night Jasmine that grew alongside the cobbled path.

The door swung open and a young, pale face peeked out from behind.

"Can I 'elp you?" The little scullery maid's eyes widened when she saw a fancy lady standing before the door, a stern expression on her face.

"I must speak with Lord Rathbone on a matter of urgency."

"Lord Rathbone's gone to bed, Ma'am," replied the astonished maid.

"Then get him up girl," replied Fenella with a wave of her hand. "He will not want to wait to hear what I have to say."

The confused little scullery maid left the door ajar and fled to the cook, who thought the matter should go to Lord Rathbone's valet. The valet thought it was something the housekeeper should deal with. She referred the matter to the butler, whose expression and tone suggested he had little interest in the matter at hand and that taking untoward house calls in the middle of the night was certainly beneath his dignity.

The matter fell back to the housekeeper, who, with rolling eyes and a scathing tongue for the scullery maid for opening the door in the first place, informed the valet that since the matter had to do with Lord Rathbone, and since he was Lord Rathbone's body servant, he should be the one to deal with it.

The valet sighed and trudged up the stairs to the doorway. To his chagrin, the woman was still there.

"His lordship does not take lady callers at night," he announced to Fenella, and started to push the door closed.

A change came over Fenella, the ruby chips in the depths of her eyes glowed and an unearthly light surrounded her for a moment. In a voice unlike her own, she said, "Lord Rathbone will wish to speak to me."

Immediately the valet threw the door open wide. "Follow me, my Lady." He led her into a warm yellow room and, asking her to sit, stoked up the fire so that it was crackling.

"Wait here just a moment, I shall ask Lord Rathbone to join you."

Lord Rathbone was not asleep. He knew he had handled matters poorly with Letty this morning. For the thousandth time he sighed, wishing that his dear wife Hannah was still with him. She would have known how to handle the matter.

It was infuriating. Nothing he did was out of anything but love for his girls. They were everything to him. Yet no matter how hard he tried, he seemed only to be able to push them further away.

The rap on his door drew him out of his reverie, but also drew his swift irritation.

"Can a man not be permitted a moment of rest in this place?" he shouted.

The valet poked his head into the room. "A thousand apologies for interrupting you, my Lord," he said, "but there is a woman downstairs you will want to see."

"What woman? Why would I want to see her at this godforsaken hour of the night?"

"I could not identify her, my Lord, but she was a woman of quality."

"If you could not identify her, how on earth would you know she was a woman of quality? No woman of quality creeps around a gentleman's house in the middle of the night seeking an audience," Lord Rathbone roared. "You should have thrown her out on the street."

"But you will want to see her, sir."

Lord Rathbone frowned suspiciously at his valet. "Have you been imbibing again, Reynolds?"

"No, my Lord." Reynolds seemed astonished. "I am perfectly sober."

"And yet you let a strange woman into my house and then insist that I see her? At an hour that is very far from civilised?"

"You will want to see her, my Lord."

It was the third time Reynolds had repeated the same sentence.

"My god I have an entire staff of imbeciles," Lord Rathbone grumbled under his breath. To the hapless valet he said, "Tell the woman I will be downstairs in ten minutes and that she will have no more than ten minutes of my time and that after that I am most likely to throw her out."

The valet smiled. "Yes, my Lord. We shall make her as comfortable as possible until you arrive."

"That's not what I said you..." But the valet had already scuttled out of sight.

With a long-suffering sigh, Lord Rathbone pulled on a pair of trousers and pulled his nightgown off over his head. He did nothing more than to tie a robe around his powerful chest – to remind the mystery woman that she was interrupting his slumber.

She had obviously done something to mesmerise his valet – the witch. What on earth could she want from an old widower like himself? Some kind of bribe or crossing her palm with silver, no doubt. A charlatan, and a bold one, to walk, never-you mind, into a gentleman's house at night.

Well, he would show her who was lord in his house.

But he also checked his hair before coming downstairs, smoothing it into a more dignified coif.

Arriving at the parlor – the only downstairs room where the candles were lit and burning brightly – he immediately saw the long, blonde hair and the swan-like neck of the lady who was seated facing away from the door.

"If you could tell me the meaning of this nocturnal incursion, Madam, you can soon be on your way and I can return to my bed."

The woman stood up and turned to face him and for a long moment, Lord Rathbone was shocked into silence.

"Well, Rath, that's hardly the welcome I expected."

Before him stood Emily Gardiner – or rather, Emily Stirling as she would come to be known. The love of his youthful life, and the woman who had slipped through his fingers.

He and Emily had been attracted at first sight and he had pursued her with all the ardour of a young man in the middle of his first romance. That was, until her father stepped in and told him in no uncertain terms that he would never countenance his daughter's alliance with a family whose money had been made in trade.

Old shame and rage still consumed Rath when he thought about it. He had never felt pressure to hide the source of his wealth – his grandfather had been a canny businessman – yet Lord Cranbooke's sneer, the scorn in his voice and his vitriolic words had left a scar on Rath's mind even now.

And Emily had scorned him as well, returning his desperately penned love letters unopened, and refusing to stand up with him when he asked her to dance. She even gave him the cut direct when he continued to pursue her.

He had sworn he would never love again, never let a female again take hold of his mind and make him crazy. Of course, several years later he had met Hannah. Their love had grown slowly, laying embers that would continue to smoulder their entire life.

And now, here was Emily, a little taller than he recalled and a little older, but still with Emily's face and Emily's smile.

But the smile was tempered with a half-frown, as if she was not sure of her welcome.

"I am pleased to see you, Rath. It has been a very long time."

"Indeed it has. Now state your business and be gone with you."

She gave a half-laugh. "Are you not even going to ask me to sit down?"

"No." He crossed his arms over his chest. "That would mean that I was offering you welcome."

"Oh, Rath," she sighed, sitting down anyway. "You need to let go of that old anger and hatred."

"Why should I?" he replied belligerently. "It has stood me in good stead over the years."

"But it is harmful, my dear. And incorrectly aimed." At Rath's raised eyebrow, Emily continued, "This is about your daughter. And my son."

Rath felt his jaw tighten. "What about them?"

"I cannot believe you are allowing our old spat to keep them apart."

"Spat? Spat, madam? Is that what you call it?" Rath uncrossed his arms and took a step toward his visitor. "Betrayal rather."

"I never betrayed you, Rath," she said rather quickly. "My father insisted I never see you again. It broke my heart."

"So much so that you were married to Patrick Stirling within the year?"

"That was not of my doing, I can assure you."

Lord Rathbone frowned. "What are you trying to say, Emily?"

"That it is beneath you to make our children suffer for something an old, dead tyrant did long ago to hurt us."

"Tyrant?"

Emily laughed uncertainly. "My father. He was the one to force us apart. He insisted that I cut you, that I marry Patrick."

"But you continued to snub me, even after you were married."

"I could not stand to see you so happy with your wife when I was so miserable with my husband."

She stood up, directly in front of Lord Rathbone.

"You see, Rath, I never stopped loving you. Not for one moment."

Lord Rathbone took a step back, his mind spinning.

Emily continued. "Please do not make the same mistake my father did."

For a moment Rath was sure her eyes turned a dark shade of blue. But Emily's eyes had always been a pure, shining green.

"Emily, I... I had no idea. You gave me no indication…"

"How could I, with guardians and chaperones and spies all about?"

Rath blinked in the low light, certain that her hair darkened several shades. It must have been the candles flickering in their sconces.

Emily stepped right up to Lord Rathbone and put a hand on his sleeve. "We cannot change the past, Rath. But you can change the future. Letty and James are perfect together. A blind man can see that."

"And how do you feel about aligning your family with one whose money was made in trade?"

"I have never felt more certain of a thing in my life. Oh!"

With a strange pop, Rath found himself standing, not before Emily, but a stranger – a tall, dark-haired woman who seemed just as surprised as he. And she had wings.

And then, in the beat of a wing, she was gone.

Rath stood stunned, feeling as if he had just awoken from a strange dream. Had it been an apparition? Was he going mad? He should have known from the start it wasn't Emily – the woman had been too tall and without Emily's mannerisms.

And yet, he could still feel the warmth of the woman's hand on his sleeve.

If it was not Emily, then who? And why? Had she appeared just to tell him that he should be kinder to James, to let him pursue his suit with Letty?

Perhaps it had been the answer to the question he had been asking. Perhaps the vision had been sent by Hannah to help him decide.

Maybe he had been too hard on James. After all, a man was not necessarily the sum of his family, no matter who his family was. And the apparition had said that Letty and James were perfect together.

Slowly, he traipsed up the stairs back to his bedroom, lost in thought. Had he become so jaded since Hannah's death that he could no longer think matters through clearly?

No, he needed no apparition to tell him what the best thing was to do.

Climbing into bed, he made a resolve to speak to Letty first thing in the morning.

Chapter Six.

"You know we can't use our magic on anyone but our godchildren, Fenella. That's basic godmothering."

Lachlan strode down the corridor at Fairy Godmother headquarters with Fenella scuttling along behind.

"But I didn't, Lachlan. I only used my magic on me."

He stopped and turned suddenly and Fenella all but bumped into him.

"That's just pedantics and you know it," he said, holding up an admonishing finger.

"No, it's legitimate," she argued. "The happily ever after was at stake."

"That's just like a dark fae. Doing something wrong then blaming everyone else except themselves."

"Don't you dare make this into a dark magic thing."

"You couldn't even sustain the glamour," Lachlan snorted. "What were you thinking, trying to imitate his past love?"

"I needed a vehicle to help him see how unreasonable he was being." She beamed at Lachlan. "And it worked. He is planning to wish Letty all happiness tomorrow morning."

Lachlan shook his head and sighed, clearly dissatisfied. "I don't know, Fenella, sometimes the end does not justify the means."

"What does that mean?"

"It means you shouldn't go sailing so close to the wind."

"You're saying a lot of nothing, Lachlan."

"I'm just trying to say – Stop flaunting the rules, Fenella."

She clicked her fingers in his face. "I care that for the rules," she said, but he caught her hand and squeezed her fingers until they hurt. She breathed in and, looking into Lachlan's eyes, found she couldn't breathe out again.

"How are you going to be one of the first dark fae godmothers if you refuse to behave? Answer me that, Miss Fenella. The rules are there for good reason. Now follow them, or I will have to take the matter before the governors." Flicking her hand away, he turned on his heel and stalked down the corridor.

Fenella massaged her hand, trying to restore feeling in her poor fingers and breath to her lungs. She glared at Lachlan's retreating figure. He couldn't possibly understand – her dark magic needed to skim the rules, or it wouldn't work. It wasn't nice and obedient like his light magic.

Although she would like to know the trick he had used to make her breathless. That might come in handy.

Besides, her plan had worked. Even if it hadn't played out exactly as she had expected it to. She should probably have researched Emily's personality a little more. And put some more energy into sustaining the image. But that was beside the point. It had worked. And now Letty's happily ever after was all but assured.

With a spring in her step, Fenella turned and skipped in the opposite direction down the corridor. It was time to watch some magic happen.

* * *

The following morning Letty's Papa came to breakfast with a subdued expression.

"Good morning Letty, good morning Clara."

"Good morning Papa," they replied in chorus, curious at the lack of color in their Papa's voice.

They were even more surprised when he asked Letty for her forgiveness.

"Of course, Papa," she replied instantly, "although I have no idea what it is you think you have done to wrong me." She stood and walked to the side table where the breakfast dishes were laid out.

He gave her a sad smile. "You are a sweet girl, Letty, very much like your mother."

Letty threw Clara a troubled glance before she replied, "Thank you, Papa. Are you quite well this morning?"

"I feel a little conflicted," he said flicking out his napkin and laying it on the table. "I fear I have done you a disservice and I am not quite certain how to undo the damage."

"What disservice Papa?" Letty fished a herring from amongst the mess of them on a plate and reached for the spoon to serve herself some eggs.

"I stopped you from seeing that young man of yours."

Letty froze, serving spoon in hand. Her heart stuttered. "You mean James?"

"Yes. James."

A single herring on her plate, Letty turned back and sat at her place at the table, her mind now fully occupied with what her father was saying.

He continued, "I think I was a little hasty in refusing my permission for the two of you to see one another."

Letty shared an astonished glance with her sister.

"Then… then I am permitted to walk out with James?"

"Yes. And dance with him. And marry him, if you so desire. You have my blessing."

Letty couldn't help asking, "What on earth has happened to effect this transformation?" Clara glared at her across the table and mouthed, "Be quiet."

But Lord Rathbone smiled and replied, "Let us just say that an old flame reminded me of something."

Letty ate her single herring in three hurried mouthfuls, hardly tasting it. A bubble of joy expanded in her chest.

"May I be excused?" she said. "I have a letter that I need to write."

"Was that sufficient breakfast for you, child?"

"Oh, Papa, I could not eat another thing!"

She stood up and threw her arms around his shoulders. "Thank goodness for old flames, whoever they are!"

His laughter rang in her ears as she skipped out of the room.

Later, Clara found her scribbling away at her writing desk.

"How does one say, 'Papa had a strange change of heart?'" Letty asked Clara. "I have started this letter several times, but there just does not seem to be a way to say it that actually seems real."

Clara grinned. "Hopefully in such a way that James believes it."

"Indeed, I am not certain how he could, since I very nearly cannot believe it myself."

"Do you think this was Fenella's work?"

Letty shrugged. "I could not say. But if it was, I can finally say I am pleased to have a fairy godmother!"

Letty ended up scrawling a joyful missive to James, explaining the situation and inviting him to join her as soon as he was able.

That afternoon, there had been no reply.

Letty was unperturbed. James was very busy with his work and had probably not seen the letter yet. He would reply as soon as he was able.

When her anxious enquiries with the butler had not elicited any good news the following morning, she sent a second letter, certain that the first must have gone astray.

There was no reply to the second letter either. And a dreadful realisation overcame Letty when Clara asked, "Why on earth would he not reply? Surely he is dying to see you as much as you are dying to see him?"

"I do believe I know the reason." Letty confided in Clara about James' nocturnal visit. "I fear he was gravely disappointed with me," she said. "But I did not realise he was quite this disappointed."

Clara nodded. "He probably expected you to have significantly more spine."

"It wasn't that," she said. "He was disappointed that I would not snub my nose at convention." She turned suddenly to Clara. "But it is not in my nature to do that."

"You always have been significantly more concerned about reputation than I have."

"I know," Letty replied gloomily. "And yet here we are, you with your court of swains, and me without the one man I actually love."

It was just at this moment that Fenella appeared, throwing pink streamers and blowing a piercing whistle in a tuneless, one-note melody that put Letty's teeth on edge.

"Congratulations!" Fenella said enthusiastically. "When can I expect an invitation to the wedding?"

"Never by the looks of things," Clara remarked.

"What?" The streamers and whistle disappeared, as did the merry expression on Fenella's face. "But everything is cleared up. You are free to marry. Your happily ever after is just over the horizon."

"Except James will not speak to me." Just saying the words brought a lump to Letty's throat and she sat down hurriedly. "I have sent two letters and he had not answered either."

"Perhaps he's busy?"

"Busy would perhaps explain the first letter, but not the second." Letty sighed. "What am I to do?"

Fenella leaned her hips against the dressing table. "I don't understand," she complained. "Everything was fine. What happened?"

"Letty refused the call to adventure," Clara piped up.

At Fenella's confused expression, Letty added, "He came to carry me off to Gretna Green and I refused."

"You refused?" Fenella was aghast. "I thought you loved him."

"I do," Letty protested.

"But not enough to go with him?"

"Society would have scorned us," she protested, although her voice weakened.

"But that wouldn't matter if you loved him well enough."

"It does matter... well, it did at the time..." Letty looked between Fenella and Clara and wilted, leaning her head on her arm on the dressing table. "Heavens, what am I to do? I am such a fool."

"It's obvious," Fenella declared. "You need to make a Grand Gesture."

"But what?" asked Letty. "And how can I make a grand gesture when he will not even acknowledge me?"

"There is an assembly tonight, right?"

A furrow appeared on Letty's forehead. "I believe so."

"Brilliant. Then I shall see you there." With that, she disappeared. Letty and Clara caught each other's eyes.

"What do you suppose she has in mind?" Clara asked.

"I am not certain," replied Letty with a nervous laugh. "And knowing Fenella, I think I am afraid to find out!"

Chapter Seven.

"I do not know how I shall comport myself," Letty commented to Clara as they arrived at the assembly beribboned and curled. "If I come across James, I very much feel as if I might flee the building."

"Just keep your chin up," advised Clara. "It appears that your fairy godmother has a plan. And while the success of her plans has been a little… shall we say, erratic, perhaps, just perhaps tonight all your dreams are about to come true."

"I hope so," sighed Letty, lifting her daffodil-colored skirts slightly to trudge up the steps of the assembly hall. "However, I cannot say that I am confident of that outcome."

Clara hugged her quickly around the shoulders and Letty felt a little better.

Miss Fenella's Fault

Her good mood was dampened when a cursory glance around the room showed James, handsome as ever in his regimentals, chatting to a group of giggling young ladies. Something jealous and proprietary entered Letty's breast.

James was hers. He had always been hers, since the first time they had looked at each other. And nothing, not society, not any concerns over reputations, was going to keep her from him.

There was a touch at her elbow. Fenella, once again in pink, stood by her shoulder.

"I have the best idea for a Grand Gesture that you have ever heard of," she confided to Letty. "Watch this."

Fenella started to weave a spell with her hands, but Letty stopped her.

"No," she said. "I know what I need to do."

She took a deep breath and, squaring her shoulders, exhaled and marched over to where James was standing.

She could feel the eyes of everyone at the assembly upon her, and her face burned. It was unheard of for a young woman to approach a young man! Scandalous! Improper! But determined, she planted herself in front of James, whose face was full of doubt and surprise.

"Good evening, Captain Stirling," Letty heard herself say. "Is it not a lovely evening? May I have this dance?"

James stared at her for long enough to make Letty begin to think she had made a dreadful mistake. The other young ladies around James tittered behind their fans, and Letty's face bloomed afresh. Her heart pounded and she forgot to breathe. Tiny beads of perspiration grew cold on her skin.

Then James answered, in a measured, serious tone.

"Are you aware of the gross impropriety of a young woman asking a gentleman to dance, Miss Rathbone?"

She swallowed convulsively; eyes wide. James seemed so formidable and stern.

"Indeed sir, however I should much prefer to face a future of permanent censure than to spend another moment without you."

The assembly seemed to hold its collective breath. Even the young ladies' fans stopped moving as they waited for James' reply.

And finally, his face broke into a delighted smile. "Ha! I knew you had it in you." He picked up Letty's hand – which she only just now noticed was shaking – and kissed it, holding eye contact and thrilling Letty to the core. "I should adore the opportunity to dance with you."

* * *

Fenella danced into Lachlan's office.

"My first Happily," she crowed. "Congratulate me."

Lachlan replied sourly, "Congratulations."

Fenella sighed, shoulders slumping. "What now?"

"Shall I list all the things you did to endanger your first happily ever after?"

"No," she replied in an airy manner. "I'm happy just to bask in the glory of my first victory." She threw Lachlan a cheeky grin before dropping into a chair. "You have to allow me a few moments, surely?"

Lachlan shook his head, unable to keep the half-smile from his face. "I suppose the lessons can wait for another day. So, how does it feel?"

"It feels incredible," Fenella stretched upward like a sinewy tiger and Lachlan felt his smile slip and his mouth open slightly as Fenella's pink blouse tightened across her chest.

With much effort, he closed his mouth and his eyes, and pushed his thoughts and feelings away.

"Lachlan? What's the matter?"

He opened his eyes to find her staring at him, blue-black eyes inquisitive and concerned. He forced a smile to his face.

"Nothing. I've just got… a bit of a headache, that's all."

"Well, in that case you should take some willow bark and lie down," she replied. "I'll leave you to it." She climbed out of her chair and, like a black-and-pink jaguar, slipped silently around the door, throwing him a quick wave as she did.

Lachlan closed his eyes again and ran a distracted hand across his forehead.

Only six more to go, he thought. *I can do it.*

And suddenly, he really did have a headache.

The End

From the Author

Thank you for reading Miss Fenella's First. I hope you enjoyed her adventures, and Letty and James' little love story.

I've always been fascinated by fairy tales. Of course, as a romance writer, they are the classic happily-ever-afters, aren't they? But what about fairy godmothers? Is there only one? Why would anyone need one? And how does one go about becoming a fairy godmother?

Those questions led to the birth of Fenella, Lachlan and a whole cadre of other fae who will appear in later novels, as well as an entire backstory of legends, lore and rules. It has been as much fun creating the fae community as it has been following Fenella's fumblings!

The second novel in the Seven Wishes series, Miss Cheswick's Charm, will be available very shortly and is available for pre-order. How can Fenella bring about a young lady's happily ever after when she's just entered into a marriage of convenience?

Go to the next page for a glimpse at that one... and I do hope you will join me in the rest of Fenella's Happily Ever Afters!

Cheers

Bree Verity

Chapter One.

At the rear of the church Fenella sat scowling at the couple at the altar, her mentor Lachlan beside her.

Had anyone turned around and stared in their direction long enough they would have seen them, but since the focus of the entire congregation was the wedding being performed, the two were all but invisible. However, if someone did stare long enough to see them, their attention would have been arrested by the differences between them. Lachlan was a blond haired, blue-eyed fae, radiating happiness and light. If one looked closely enough, one would see his featherlight wings, white and mostly transparent, flapping slowly behind him. Fenella, with her jet-black hair, deathly pale skin and somber bearing, seemed to somehow dim the light around her. Animals would hiss and growl in her direction and disappear from her presence as fast as their paws could carry them. Her wings were multicolored, like a dragonfly, but just as translucent as Lachlan's. Both of them were stunningly beautiful in their own way, as were all fae - Lachlan, classically handsome and Fenella, more like a devastating and dangerous predator. Both of them wore pink - Fenella a neat, dusky pink morning dress, Lachlan in pale pink tails with a pink vest and a pink carnation in his lapel. His pale top hat also featured a pink band and his cane bore a pink ribbon. Every time Fenella glanced over at him; she couldn't help but think how ridiculous he looked. So, she kept her eyes on the wedding.

"I suppose that's it then?" Her voice held the lilt of an Irish brogue, and deep disappointment. The couple at the altar exchanged the chaste kiss that would seal their union and Fenella slumped down in her pew. "How long has it been since someone has failed to provide a happily ever after, Lachlan? I'll be famous." The sarcasm was heavy in her voice.

"More like infamous," Lachlan joked, a twinkle in his eye and a similar lilt in his voice. "But never fear, my dear, all is not yet lost. I am here to save the day." From somewhere behind him Lachlan produced a crossbow-like contraption. It seemed to be made out of solidified air, with two sharp arrows at the ready.

"Ugh." Fenella grimaced and waved her hand in front of her face, wrinkling her nose. "That thing stinks of love. What is it?"

"Just a little something that I borrowed from Cupid." Lachlan aimed the crossbow carefully. "Watch this." He pressed the release, and the two arrows went careening toward the newly wedded couple. The contraption disappeared out of Lachlan's hands.

Unfortunately, the new Mrs. Longshore and her erstwhile husband chose exactly that moment to turn away from each other and the first arrow landed with a light twang in the breast of the clergyman, who staggered backward, a hand on his heart and a surprised look on his face. The arrow vanished.

"That could be awkward." Lachlan leaned sideways toward Fenella. "Do Church of England clergy take a vow of celibacy?"

"I don't know." Fenella watched as the second arrow, its original target lost, wandered aimlessly for a moment before smacking into the breast of the middle-aged organist. She too grasped at her chest and then her surprise turned to bliss when her gaze fell upon the clergyman.

"I hope she isn't already married," Fenella said in an aside to Lachlan. He scratched his face, a worried expression crossing his features.

"Let's get out of here." Taking Fenella's hand, they winked out of view, only to reappear a moment later beside the decorated open carriage that would take

Theodore and Caroline Longshore to their wedding breakfast. The couple appeared in the doorway of the church, and Lachlan, after examining them for a moment, said in some surprise, "I don't know what it is you're worrying about."

"What?"

"Can't you see it?"

"See what?"

"The truth. In their auras."

Fenella stared at Caroline and Theodore for a moment then replied in a frustrated tone, "I can't see anything. Only the dark parts. Which, I can tell you, are not auspicious at all. Stubbornness, temper, recalcitrance… it's all there."

"Come on Fenella. You're a quarter light fae you know. Try harder."

"I am trying harder," she snapped back at Lachlan, "and I'm fairly certain that there isn't a single light fae bone in my entire body." She squinted irritatedly at the couple, trying to see what it was Lachlan saw.

He clicked his fingers. "I've got it," he crowed, winking out for a moment, reappearing with a pair of garish pink-framed eyeglasses. "Put these on."

She crossed her arms over her chest. "No thank you."

He took a stern tone. "Put them on Fenella."

"I would rather walk barefoot over a pit of boiling glass." She looked at the offending glasses with distaste. "They have to be the most hideous fashion accessory I have ever seen."

"They're rose colored glasses," explained Lachlan patiently. "They should work to suppress your awareness of the dark parts of the auras and improve your awareness of the light." He placed them on Fenella's face, expertly avoiding her flailing arms as she tried to stop him doing so. "Stop being such a baby. It's not as if anyone can see you." With a shake of his head, he took her by the shoulders and turned her to face the happy couple. "Do you see it now?"

Fenella stared for a moment, watching the couple as they ran through the crowd, crouching a little against the handfuls of rice thrown at them, and mounted the carriage. "I think I do," she said slowly, twisting her head sideways. "A little green around the edge there, and a pink hue surrounding the both of them." She turned to Lachlan and stared at him open-mouthed for several second straight, then hurriedly removed the glasses. "What does it mean?"

Lachlan chuckled. "It means they are perfect for each other. But they are both stubborn, very sure of their own opinions, and unwilling to forgive. Your job will be to make sure they appreciate each other's good qualities before they have too much exposure to the bad."

Fenella looked relieved. "So, I can still bring about her happily ever after?"

"Without a doubt."

"Wonderful." She smiled widely; an expression returned by Lachlan. "I shall go and visit Caroline this very afternoon."

"Good."

"But Lachlan?" He turned to her, questioning. "Remind me never to look at you again through those rose-colored glasses. You are so sickly sweet you nearly made me return my breakfast."

And with that, they winked out of sight.

Like it? Miss Cheswick's Charm is available for pre-order on Amazon.

One Last Thing…

If you enjoyed this story, it would be awesome if you could leave a review somewhere – Amazon, Kobo, Goodreads, your own blog… Reviews for indie writers are almost as good as money… almost…

Thanks so much! You rock.

Milton Keynes UK
Ingram Content Group UK Ltd.
UKHW030025180324
439604UK00001B/90